Earth vs the Star Mummy

Lucas Mangum

Less Than Pulp Books

Book Cover by Christy Aldridge

1st edition 2022

Contents

For the weirdoes...

1

"There you are, you fucking square," someone said from the entrance to Marty's Malt Shop. The door banged shut behind the vulgar entrant. Andrew McCready looked up from his burger and fries to face the door and saw Tommy Castle standing there in his leather jacket and blue jeans. His hair was greased back, and he grinned his signature grin. It was an expression that told Andrew and anyone else who might see it that the Castle Boy was up to no good. He seldom was up to anything wholesome; it was part of what made him interesting. He continued, "I've been looking all over for your sorry ass."

"I won't have that kind of language inside my shop," Marty said from behind the counter in a voice gone gruff with age and too many cigarettes. "Take it in the streets where it belongs, yeah?"

Tommy went from chest-puffing bravado to schoolboy charm, folding his hands in front of him and softening his expression.

"Sorry, Mr. Marty. No disrespect. I'm just excited. See..." He made a show of looking around at the other patrons. There were maybe a half-dozen people inside the establishment, not counting Marty or his staff. Most were enjoying meals not unlike Andrews'. A few did seem to perk up a little. Tommy was the bad boy in Conestoga, New Mexico, and just about everyone knew it. People claimed not to like him—some did genuinely hate his guts—but all liked hearing about whatever he was up to; it gave them something to gossip about. He said in a near-whisper, "... something fell from the sky out by Route 63. Just like that shit that happened in Roswell a few years back."

"Damn it, Tommy. What did I tell you about that filth?"

Andrew tried not to snicker at Marty breaking his own rule.

"Right. Sorry. Anyway, I wanted to see if my pal McCready here wanted to come check it out with me." Tommy faced Andrew, that mischievous grin back on his face. "Well, what do you say? Not chicken, are you?"

Andrew searched his thoughts. He wasn't scared, per se, but a night out with Tommy Castle hadn't been on the agenda for him, and he usually had to prepare himself for such misadventures. Still, the idea of an object from space falling just outside the limits of his town got him pretty excited, even if it turned out just to be a meteorite. Before he could answer in the affirmative, his stomach grumbled and reminded him why he'd come to Marty's in the first place. He'd just finished a long day on his family's ranch and worked up quite an appetite.

"I'm in the middle of a meal," he said, nodding down at his plate.

"If what you say is true, maybe going to check it out ain't such a hot idea." That was Alice, the only server on staff tonight. She had paused in the middle of the floor after a round of refilling coffees to hear Tommy out. She still had the mostly empty carafe clutched in her bejeweled fingers. People said she wore too many rings, but Andrew thought her style was pretty bitchin'. Worlds different than everyone else in town. "I've heard things about those Unidentified Flying whatever they are," she said. "Scary things."

More people looked up to watch the interaction unfold. Some murmured among themselves in excited tones.

"Oh, don't worry your pretty little head," Tommy said. "I've got Kelly Ford with me, and he brought his daddy's shotgun."

"Does Kelly's daddy *know* you have his shotgun?" Marty asked. "Don't think he'd be too pleased."

Tommy ignored him and kept his attention on Alice. She was approaching thirty and could've almost been his mother if she'd had him extra young, but that never stopped him from flirting. She'd never had a husband as far as anyone knew, and even if she did, it was unlikely such a minor speed bump would discourage one Tommy Castle. Andrew had heard rumors about Tommy and older women, attached and otherwise.

"You're welcome to come along too," he said. "Bet you'd be a real sight for sore eyes if there are any... passengers... on board."

She blushed and fluffed her hair with her free hand. "Well, I..."

"You're not off until ten, Alice," Marty reminded her.

Her cheeks flushed a deeper shade of pink. "Right."

"Besides, you heard scary things, remember?"

"Right," she said again and headed to the back.

"And spacemen aren't real," Marty said to Tommy.

Without missing a beat, Tommy looked at Andrew again.

"Well, that leaves you, buckaroo. You can eat those fries on the road, come on."

"Is that okay, Marty?" Andrew asked.

Marty sighed. He liked Andrew well enough and had told Andrew as much. He'd also told Andrew that he didn't understand why a nice young man like him hung around with a hooligan like Tommy. Andrew never had an answer, at least not one he thought Marty would want to hear. Truthfully, there was something exciting about Tommy Castle, in the same way he found Alice's fashion sense intriguing. Tommy was different than everyone else in town, including Andrew himself. Every person in Conestoga seemed content to live and die in Conestoga, working for their parents or some other local shop, whereas Tommy had a mind for adventure and spontaneity. He was just the type of guy to bring friends with him to go searching for some fallen hunk of space debris. Or whatever had crashed out by Route 63.

"Fine by me," Marty said, "so long as you pay up before you go."

"Yes, of course. How much do I owe you?"

"Buck and a half will square us."

Andrew reached into his pocket and tossed the money on the counter.

"I appreciate it," he said and got up from his stool, clutching the greasy paper containing his food to his chest like a deflated football.

"And you kids best be safe, you hear?" Marty said.

"Always, Mr. Marty, always," Tommy said with a mocking bow, and with that, he and Andrew left the malt shop.

Outside, Tommy's DeSoto Firedome idled beside the curb. It was a sleek, black machine that Tommy liked to boast could outrace any other car in town on any given day of the week. Twice on Sunday, he always liked to add.

He also bragged that he'd bought it with his own money, saved from those summers he worked as a courier for his old man's greeting card business, but rumor had it he'd gotten the wheels as a gift from an extremely well-off uncle, some hot shot movie producer who lived in Palm Springs.

On weekends, anyone driving past the Castle residence at the right hour might spot Tommy giving the car a nice, thorough cleaning, caressing it with suds and wax like one might caress a woman with tanning oil at the beach.

Kelly lounged in the passenger seat of Tommy's prized set of wheels with a smoldering cigarette pinched between his pale fingers. A can of

Schlitz rested between his legs. The shotgun was laid across the floor in the back, next to a case of the beer.

"Ready to go hunting for Martians?" Kelly said. His demeanor lacked the deviousness of Tommy's and any sense of excitement. But that was Kelly. He only seemed to have one gear, like he was always coasting, never in a rush, but never stalled out, either. Andrew envied him a little in that way. Kelly very well could have been excited about "Martian hunting," as he called it, but he didn't show it the way Tommy did.

Andrew got into the car, not sure what to think. On the one hand, it was highly unlikely that anything that had fallen from the sky would harbor some intelligent life—and maybe that was a good thing—but they might find something cool, maybe even something that could make them rich. On the other hand, Tommy and Kelly could be pulling his chain about the whole thing. It wouldn't be the first time they tried to get one over on him for a laugh.

"I'm Walking Behind You" played low on the stereo. It was a nearly inescapable tune. Andrew heard it at home while helping his mom clean, at Marty's on the juke, and on the radio whenever he got into someone's car. It was a bona fide hit and had a nice melody to it, but he sure would like to hear something else every once in a while.

Tommy revved the engine. The Firedome made a guttural sound, like a waking beast. He shifted into gear and pulled away from Marty's Malt Shop. Andrew watched the restaurant grow smaller in the rearview until they turned on Santa Rosa, removing his favorite spot to eat from his line of sight.

This little excursion probably wouldn't amount too much, but it might be good for a few kicks.

He took a big bite of his burger and grabbed one of the beers to wash it down.

Never once did he think this might be his last meal.

2

They drove out to the edge of town where Main met Route 63. Over the desert, the sky appeared to have more stars than empty black space. The lack of light pollution made visibility crystal clear and looking up at the night sky out here always gave Andrew a feeling he couldn't quite describe, something that said to him that no matter what the priest said on Sundays at Saint Gregory's, Andrew, and everyone else was alone, insignificant, and ignorant about too many things to count. It was both a freeing and frightening sensation, one which kept him awake on more nights than it didn't. Certainly, more often than he would dare admit to Tommy, Kelly, or his parents.

"Where'd you say it was?" Kelly asked.

"Down the road apiece," Tommy said. "Two, maybe three mile markers."

"And you're sure you saw it?"

It was Andrew's third time asking. This wasn't how he'd planned on spending tonight. He'd hoped to finish his meal at the malt shop and then walk over to Jessica Walker's house to throw pebbles at her bedroom window until she came out to see him. They could've sat on her roof, looking up at the stars, and maybe done a little necking. Jessica was a real dolly, but Tommy's proposal had been too intriguing. Andrew would be real ticked off if this turned out to be a whole lotta nothing or just another joke at his expense.

"I told you, McCready. I saw something. It was big and green, and it fell from the sky. That's all I know. What's got you so worked up, anyway?"

He shook his head. "Tired, I guess."

He could *not* tell Tommy about Jessica. She had told him not to mention their dalliances to anyone, but especially not to Tommy. He would never let her (or anyone else) hear the end of it.

"You say we girls talk too much, but that Tommy's a real chatter-box," she liked to say. "And he never met a bit of gossip he didn't like. Tell him about us and we're not just through; you're dead."

Andrew took her threat very seriously. She had brothers in the military and a dad who used to be a prizefighter.

Kelly took another Schlitz from the case at Andrew's feet. He glanced at the shotgun, then at Andrew's face.

"If things get hairy, do you know how to use that thing?"

Andrew gulped. "I... I mean, I've fired a handgun."

Tommy laughed like he'd just heard the world's funniest joke. It was a high-pitched, feral sound. Andrew was surprised more people didn't give Tommy any grief for it. It sounded ridiculous, like a hyena in heat.

"Maybe we should let Kelly do the shooting," Tommy said.

"It's all right," Kelly said. "You just rack, point, and shoot."

Andrew didn't feel even a little at ease. Kelly must have picked up on it because he added, "But yeah, just leave it to me."

Another uncomfortable beat passed where the only sound was the purr of the engine. Kelly concluded, "It's probably just a meteor or something, anyway."

"Hey, we're here!" Tommy said and slowed the Firedome to a crawl.

Andrew looked out the window as the tires hit the roadside gravel, kicking plumes of dust into the night air.

"I don't see anything," he said and again thought of Jessica Walker. He could be on her roof right now, holding hands and kissing, maybe doing a little more. Instead, he was out in the desert with these two dopes. "Where is it?"

The Firedome rolled to a stop, and Tommy cut the engine.

"Keep your pants on, McCready. It's a few paces out yonder." He flashed that grin of his. "Maybe carry the beer if you can't shoot."

"You're a real jerk, you know that?" Andrew said.

"Ladies, ladies," Kelly said in his easy way. He reached for the shotgun and fed it into the front seat. He flashed a brief, subtle smile. "Let's hunt some Martians."

Once they were out of the car, Andrew could see something about a hundred paces away from the side of the road. It looked like smoke from a campfire, but people weren't supposed to camp out here. It wasn't legal, and it probably wasn't safe. Too many snakes, scorpions, and coyotes lurking about in the sand. They were more likely to need the shotgun for an encounter with the local wildlife than any Martians. Andrew was glad they'd brought it.

"Is that it?" he asked, pointing toward the smoke column.

"I think so," Tommy said, switching on a flashlight.

Andrew detected a hint of reservation in his voice. Kelly must have noticed it, too, because he exchanged a glance with Andrew. In the dark, it was hard to read Kelly's expression, but he imagined puzzlement in it. Surely Tommy wasn't pulling both their legs.

The three young men drew closer to the billowing smoke. When they reached the halfway point between it and the road, Andrew noticed something funny about it.

"You guys see that?" he asked. "It's green."

"Didn't I say it was green?" Tommy said.

"I guess I thought you made that part up."

"Why would I do that?"

"I never heard of green shooting stars, have you?" Kelly asked.

It was like he'd read Andrew's mind.

"Maybe coming out here wasn't such a hot idea," Andrew said, wanting to kick himself for not saying it back at Marty's, wishing he was up on Jessica's roof.

"Don't be such a chicken," Tommy said, all reservation now gone from his voice.

Kelly racked the shotgun without even thinking about it. They were nearly at the crash site.

The smoke was thicker than normal smoke, and it had a strange glow to it.

"Anyone else smell that?" Kelly asked.

Andrew took a big whiff and wished he hadn't.

"God, that's awful," he said. "What is that?"

"Smells like formaldehyde."

Tommy covered his mouth with a handkerchief and trod forward. The odd-colored vapor enshrouded him as he stood over the crater.

"Well, I'll be a..." he trailed off.

Andrew and Kelly stuttered to a stop beside him. Kelly lowered the rifle. All the moisture dried in Andrew's mouth.

"It's one of those mummy coffins," Tommy said.

"A sarcophagus," Andrew managed to croak.

The container had smooth, gray edges. Andrew couldn't tell if the material was stone or some kind of metal; it looked like some combination of the two. A face with feminine features was carved into the surface of the object's head.

Kelly gestured with the gun. "There's something inscribed on its chest."

Using his handkerchief, Tommy bent to wipe away the debris from the inscription.

"It's in those, what're they called, hyper-glyphics," he said.

"Hieroglyphics," Andrew said. "But they don't look Egyptian."

"I wonder what they say," Tommy said, and scrubbed at the sarcophagus's sculpted face.

A sudden ooh sound made him jump back. He released his flashlight, and it clattered against the shell of the sarcophagus before going dark. The sound continued, reminding Andrew of a cross between a ghost and something electronic. It warbled and buzzed, shifting its pitch at seemingly random intervals.

"What is that?" Kelly said. Gone was his usual dry tone. His voice wavered with dreadful uncertainty.

Andrew instinctively covered his ears, but his hands did little to muffle the steady flow of sound waves. The notes fogged his brain, making him feel like he'd just awakened from a deeply troubled sleep.

The gray skin of the vessel began to change color, taking on a bright yellow hue, outlined with the same green as the smoke. Every fiber of Andrew's being told him that he and the others should run back to the car and drive back into town, forgetting this ever happened, but he couldn't move. Tommy and Kelly were similarly transfixed by the unfolding strangeness, apparently frozen where they stood.

An abrupt hiss brought an end to the bizarre noise, and the coffin darkened back to gray. The boys looked at each other. None of them could find the right words. This was so outside their realm of experience, so unbelievable.

The lid of the sarcophagus yawned open, expelling a thicker gust of green smoke and a headier whiff of formaldehyde. Andrew's eyes watered, and he felt a little nauseous. When the smoke cleared, he and the others let out a collective gasp.

"It's a mummy," Andrew said.

"Yeah, from space!" Tommy added.

"We should go," Kelly said. "Something's not right."

Tommy twisted his face in exasperation. "Are you kidding? This is the discovery of the century. I bet the college will pay a pretty penny for this, and we found it. Hell, I bet the government will give us a medal."

Andrew tended to agree with Kelly more than Tommy on this one, but he couldn't bring himself to turn and leave. He needed to keep looking, needed to confirm he was really seeing this, and not dreaming or gone mad from breathing in that green smoke. Kelly couldn't bring himself to leave either; he stayed put, but he did raise his rifle.

"What are you guys worried about, anyway?" Tommy said. "Newsflash: mummies are dead, or do you believe everything you see in the movies?"

He reached into the crater to grab his flashlight.

A bandaged hand grabbed his wrist.

3

At first, Kelly thought it might be a joke. It was just like Tommy Castle to reach next to a mummy and scream like it had grabbed him. But then, the skin on his face and neck began to bubble and hiss like hot soup. Steam radiated from his flesh and mixed with the green smoke that hung about them. The smell reminded Kelly of sausages cooking in an ungreased pan.

The figure from inside the space coffin rose, holding fast to Tommy—Tommy, whose screams had liquefied like he was gargling something thick and syrupy. When one of the bulging masses on Tommy's face burst, expelling blood and chunky yellow bits, Kelly remembered the gun in his hands. He pointed it at the living mummy and fired. The buckshot flared and made yellow-green sparks when it burst against the bandaged flesh, but the mummy seemed otherwise unaffected. It simply released Tommy, causing his remains to splatter and thump into the sarcophagus.

There was little of him left that resembled something human. His leather jacket and jeans hung off a lumpy, wet mass that was topped with a shock of stringy, gummy hair.

Someone else was screaming now, and Kelly couldn't tell if it was Andrew or himself.

The mummy faced him, bandages falling away from its face to reveal the most stunning woman he'd ever laid eyes on. Sure, there were plenty of babes in town, but the face under the bandages was downright exotic, like something even his wildest fantasies couldn't hope to conjure. With flowing black hair, a piercing gaze, and a strong jawline, she was a warrior queen straight out of the pulps, embodied in exquisite flesh.

Only, this dream girl from the stars had just murdered his friend.

He took aim again, this time pointing right at the mummy's otherworldly, beautiful face.

Another flash of that eerie green burst from her eyes before he could shoot. The gun went hot in his hands, and he let go. It disintegrated with a mechanical sizzle before it could hit the desert floor. Aside from the heat in the palms, the rifle left no trace.

The mummy lifted her right hand, and the bandages snaked forward, ensnaring Kelly's wrists. The material was hot on his skin—even hotter than the vaporizing gun. The pressure came on quick and was powerful enough to cut off the circulation to his hands. He cried out—certain now that these were his screams—as the bandages dragged him across the sand, putting him on a collision course with this beastly, alien beauty. As he slid closer, the bandages unraveled from her and wrapped themselves around more parts of him, setting his nerve endings afire with agony, and fracturing his mind with the madness of sheer terror.

Andrew turned to run. It was the only thing that made sense after Tommy melted and the now-naked mummy turned her attention from the fully bandaged Kelly to him. He pumped his legs. He screamed for help, even though he was the only human soul nearby. Breath after ragged breath tore through his lungs. Up ahead, the Firedome didn't seem to be getting any closer.

He skidded to a halt when two yellow eyes materialized in the dark. He'd been running so fast that the sudden stop sent him spilling to his rump. The impact kicked up a cloud of sand that made it difficult to see. He waved his hands to try clearing the air quicker and saw he was face to face with a coyote. Its hackles were raised, and it was baring its teeth.

"Oh, God!" he cried.

It wasn't the only animal in his path. There were two other coyotes, one on either side of him. In the spaces between them, smaller night critters moved in the shadowy sands. Andrew whimpered, knowing the shapes had to be spiders, scorpions, or snakes—maybe even all three. Behind him, the mummy's bare feet gently padded toward him.

With a yelp, he scooted and faced her. She didn't quicken her approach. The moonlight reflected blue off her nude form. This close to him, she didn't smell like formaldehyde at all, but some exotic spice, something not of this world.

She stood over him. All around him, the creatures of the night growled and crept and slithered.

She reached for him, touching his cheek with a hand as cool as stone. Without words, she ushered him to his feet. He continued to whine, though he no longer felt any reservations about being in this alien presence. He parted his lips, and she breathed into him.

With this breath, his life took on a new purpose.

4

Jessica Walker jolted awake when a pebble plinked against her bedroom window. She'd been having one of her water dreams again. In this one, water of the most vibrant blue had filled a desert canyon. On the previously dry and sandy slopes, lush green foliage had blossomed. Jessica floated in this new majestic river, taking in the sights. Dreams like this brought her an incredible sense of peace, and they only came when she was in the deepest of sleeps.

She blinked to clear the cobwebs from her sleepy head and reached over to turn on the bedside lamp. In the new illumination, with the images of that water-filled canyon fading from her mind, she saw it was after midnight. Another pebble tapped her window and tumbled to the overhang below.

"Oh, for Pete's sake," she groaned.

If this was Andrew, he'd better have a good explanation for coming by so late, she thought. He was probably hitting the Schlitz too hard tonight. That Tommy Castle really was no good. He was a lousy kisser, too, or at least that was what she'd heard from Joy Milton.

Jessica rolled out of bed and stuffed her feet into her slippers. Another pebble hit her window as she shuffled toward it, which only annoyed her further.

She reached for the glass and undid the latch, ready to give her late-night caller a piece of her mind.

"All right, Mister," she growled and threw open the window, but when she saw Andrew standing on her lawn, her train of thought derailed. A wet blanket of worry stifled her ire at being awakened at this ungodly hour. "Andrew?"

He didn't respond. He only stood there with his shoulders slightly stooped and leaning slightly to one side. Maybe it was the moonlight, but there was something wrong with his face, too. It looked like he'd smeared it with blue chalk.

What's wrong with him?

She thought about getting her father, but that would start a whole world of trouble she did not want to navigate right now.

Should I call for a doctor?

She decided she'd better see what was wrong first. Getting an ambulance or the police involved sounded like a headache too, especially if this was some kind of joke.

"Wait there," she said. "I'll be right down."

Andrew remained slack-jawed, staring, and silent. She made to turn and get her coat, but she added, "You better not be horsing around!"

No response. She huffed and shook her head and then got her coat. She took the steps as lightly as possible. Usually, she had Andrew climb up the side of her house, but he didn't look like he was in any condition to do that tonight. She kept her breathing slow and quiet, so as not to wake her father. At the door, she stopped to listen for sounds of him getting out of bed. Once sure he was undisturbed, she lightly turned the doorknob and stepped outside.

Andrew looked even worse up close. That pale blue stuff wasn't just on his face; it was on his arms and neck too. It might not have even been on his skin, but in his skin. She couldn't totally tell in the dark.

"Andrew?" she said. "What's wrong with you?"

He held out his hand. He was breathing, but it sounded dry and raspy, the way Marty at the Malt Shop sounded whenever he overexerted himself. Old Marty's breath never smelled like this, though; Andrew's smelled like he had been chugging cleaning supplies or something all night. Was it really strong liquor? Or worse, drugs?

"Andrew, if my dad comes out here and sees you like this, you're gonna be in big trouble."

He didn't react to her threat at all. Normally, any mention of her father made his eyes widen with an almost childlike panic, but tonight, he just stood there, holding out his hand and breathing like a sick dog. Jessica opened her mouth to ask again what was wrong, but Andrew spoke first.

"Shhhhheeeee," he wheezed.

The single, drawn-out syllable turned her blood to a raw, hyperthermic liquid.

"What?"

"Sheee's comiiinnggg."

"Who?" Jessica shook her head, a spike of anger jabbing through all curiosity and dread. "Hey, what the hell is this all about, huh? Tommy, are you out here? Did you put him up to this? I'm telling you, it's not funny!"

"Submit," Andrew said in a grainy whisper. "Submit or beeee destroooyyyed."

Jessica opened her mouth to protest further, but then Andrew's face contorted as if he meant to yell—it was an expression she'd seen countless times on the faces of her father and brothers. No sound emerged from him beyond the dry wheezing, though, and his features continued to contort. His face looked like paper crumpled by an unseen hand as his cheeks collapsed into his open mouth, his nose caved in, and his eyeballs sank deep into his skull. The same rapid decay was happening elsewhere on his body, too. Anywhere he had skin, he dried up and decomposed.

All the while, Jessica tried to determine what could be causing it and what she should do. This was something beyond comprehension, completely alien to her short, small-town life. It was frightening, but also so baffling, she couldn't even manage to scream. She could only watch and try to make sense of these events as they unfolded.

Andrew's skeleton collapsed in her front yard, still wearing his shirt and trousers. She watched as the bones disintegrated and a sudden, stiff breeze carried the blue dust to the west.

Only his clothes remained. They looked as if someone had simply discarded them for some unknown reason and run naked into the night.

Jessica's bottom lip trembled. Andrew's raspy warning echoed in her mind.

Sheee's comiiinnggg.

This had to be a dream. She was still sleeping and would wake up any minute now. Probably with Andrew throwing pebbles at her window. They'd go up on her roof and watch the stars, just like they always did. Maybe she'd let him get a little farther with her tonight than normal. He was a good guy and hadn't told anyone about their secret meetings. Not even his jerk-o-zoid best friend Tommy Castle.

She took two steps back, trepidation in each motion. Any sudden action, she feared, would crumble the world further and make this nightmare inescapable.

A heavy hand fell on her shoulder, and the scream that she couldn't quite find the breath to expel mere seconds ago finally escaped her. It was a high, sharp screech that gouged its way through the quiet night.

5

Earth vs the Star Mummy *will be back after a word from our sponsor.*

Carl and Carli sit in a DeSoto Firedome on a cliff overlooking a city at night. "I'm Walking Behind You" plays low on the stereo. Carl drapes his arm over the seat behind Carli's head.

"How'd you like the movie, Carli?" Carl asks.

"It was fine, Carl, just fine."

Carli sighs and fiddles with a lock of her hair.

"How do you like me?" he asks.

Carli giggles. They move toward each other for a kiss. Carl opens his mouth. With a burst of static, the song cuts off. Carli's face twists in disgust, and she pulls away.

"You're not gonna kiss her after that burger with extra onions from Marty's Malt Shop, are you, Carl?" a voice from the radio scolds.

Carl faces forward, making an expression of adorably innocent dejection, and nods at the camera.

"Well, then you need..." A triumphant musical motif makes the pause more dramatic. "... Lucas's Man Gum, the only gum to make you feel like a man (and she'll see you as one too)."

A pale hand holding a white rectangle of gum pops out of the dashboard.

"Chew on this, stud, and she won't be able to resist your luscious lips, even after a burger with extra onions from Marty's."

"Thanks, Lucas," Carl says, and lets the hand from the dashboard feed him the stick.

Carl chews while Carli sits with her face still frozen in a mask of revulsion. Carl's face lights up.

"Mmmm," he declares. "Man Gum."

He grins and faces Carli again. She smiles too.

"Much better," she says.

The song on the stereo comes back on, swelling in volume as Carl and Carli mash their lips together.

Up next, the Sonnet Productions Triple Feature Horror Show continues with Earth vs the Lava Spiders, *an eruption of pyroclastic, arachnoid thrills from the terrifying imagination of Candace Nola, immediately following* Earth vs the Star Mummy.

We now return to Earth vs the Star Mummy.

6

The Army jeep swerved out of control. Its shredded back bumper dragged on the pavement of Yucca Flats Boulevard, throwing bright sparks into the air. The dead wheelman leaned out the driver's side window with his face blackened and most of his hair singed off. The passenger frantically fumbled for the steering wheel but could find no purchase. Somewhere nearby, people were screaming. Gunfire cracked through the air like angry thunder.

The jeep crashed into the windowed facade of Murphy's Drug, exploding the glass apart like translucent fireworks. It bumped to a stop with half its body lodged into the jagged maw it made in the front of the store. The passenger scrambled to escape, but with a loud concussion, the jeep burst into flames.

"It's a fucking war zone out there," Marty said, and no one called him a hypocrite for using profanity in his place of business.

Alice knew it all would go to hell when those military vehicles pulled in the day after Tommy Castle walked into the malt shop and said something fell from the sky beside Route 63. She'd had her fears about where things would go that night, even.

She had tossed and turned, thinking about a flick she caught at the drive-in a few years back. It was called *The Day the Earth Stood Still*. In the film, a flying saucer lands in Washington, D.C., carrying an alien named Klaatu and his robot companion named Gort. Concerned about Earth's aggression after the discovery of rockets and atomic energy, they have an urgent message for humanity: be peaceful or be obliterated by an alliance of interstellar forces.

As someone who lived in the state where the first nuclear bomb was detonated, Alice found the movie incredibly unsettling. It disturbed her even more when she considered the alleged alien visitation that took place in Roswell only two short years later. Roswell wasn't too far from Conestoga, and the other night, she got wondering if her whole state had become some hotbed for alien activity. Maybe it was like the movie said, and visitors from the stars considered humanity hostile. The whole species had been deemed a plague that must be eradicated.

The passenger of the Army jeep emerged from the damaged storefront of Murphy's Drug. Fully engulfed in flames, he screamed and flailed, staggering across the street.

"He's headed this way!" she yelled.

"What do we do?" one of the customers asked. That was Josiah Smith. He was a regular, coming every morning for breakfast and asking for the same order of French toast he'd had since Marty opened the place. Extra powdered sugar, extra syrup, and no cinnamon. He had a paunch, salt-and-pepper hair, and always dressed like he'd come from church, even in the hottest months of summer. "We can't let him in here," he hollered.

The passenger fell against the front door. His charred skin left black smears on the glass as he slumped to his knees, still burning.

"We gotta put him out or the heat's gonna break that glass," Alice said, rushing to the kitchen to grab the fire extinguisher. She came out with it. Marty followed her dutifully to the door. She pulled the pin. "On three," she said.

She counted and took a deep breath. She held it while Marty opened the door. A plume of smoke billowed inside and some of the customers groaned with disgust from the stink of burning meat. She sprayed the flames with the extinguisher, telling herself to treat it like just another kitchen fire, nothing more.

Outside, but frightfully nearby, more gunfire popped through the air. Marty shut the door on the smoking form of the soldier without bothering to check for a pulse. Alice looked at the glass door and the multiple windows.

"We're not safe here," she said.

No one disagreed.

"Hey, Mummy-bitch!" Lanny Walker got into an orthodox fighting stance in the middle of Santa Rosa.

The night he'd found his daughter hysterical on his front lawn with the McCready boy's threads piled before her, he would've found the idea of reanimated mummies, let alone reanimated mummies from space, downright preposterous. Lanny Walker believed in what he could see and touch. A man who'd once made a decent living with his fists, he placed his faith firmly in the tactile. He didn't even believe in God, despite accompanying his family to St. Gregory's every Sunday—a man had to be supportive of his family, even if that meant swallowing his pride and keeping certain views of his hidden.

Now, with this Star Mummy wreaking havoc in Conestoga, not only could he say he fully believed everything Jessica said that night, but he could also get a chance to fight for something. It had been far too long since he could say that, and he relished the opportunity to use his fists again.

"Hey!" he shouted again.

"Lanny, what the fuck?"

That was Arty Boyer, hiding behind the nearest dumpster like a fat coward like him would do in a situation like this. Arty was his boss at the Conestoga Mining Company and a real blowhard. He loved acting tough when he had the power and even pushed Lanny around, knowing the former prizefighter wouldn't dare slug him when he so desperately needed the work. Now, though, Lanny wouldn't be surprised if the prick had soiled himself.

"I'm talking to you, Mummy-bitch!" Lanny took two steps forward, while still maintaining his fighter's stance.

The Mummy-bitch in question was levitating above the street several feet ahead. Wrapped in bandages everywhere but her head, she'd just laser-eyed a cop car, causing it to flip upside down and burst into green flames. The men inside squealed as their flesh cooked.

Lanny spotted an empty beer bottle in the gutter and bent to pick it up.

"This'll get your attention," he muttered and hurled the bottle at the back of her head.

It struck her and shattered. The impact garnered her attention but didn't stagger her. That was okay. The distance must have lessened the blow. If she got close enough, he'd knock her block off. He didn't hit women as a rule, but here, he could make an exception.

The Star Mummy faced him and smirked.

"That's right," he said. "A proper fight's what you want. Come on!"

One of her coyote minions leapt at him from a nearby window. He dropped the beast with a right cross and laughed.

"I want you, Mummy-bitch, not your pets."

The smirk on her face remained. She began to lower herself.

"Lanny, this is a bad idea!"

The two women and other man hiding behind the dumpster nodded and grunted their assent.

It's the end of the world, and everyone's still kissing Arty's pimply, fat ass, he thought ruefully.

"Shut up, Arty," Lanny said out of the corner of his mouth.

The Star Mummy's bandaged feet touched the pavement.

Lanny stepped around a swollen, blotchy-skinned corpse that was crawling with tarantulas and other spiders. The Star Mummy walked toward him at a confident pace. He kept his hands up, ready to hit anything she dared throw in his way. She didn't see him as a threat, and she would pay dearly for that.

"To hell with this!" the second man behind the dumpster said.

He got up and took off down Santa Rosa. The Star Mummy flicked her head slightly to the right and sent a burst of green from her eyes. The lasers blasted a smoking hole in the back of the man's head. He crumbled to his knees, and then to his face. One of the women shrieked.

The mummy returned her attention to Lanny.

"That's right. Eyes on the prize, baby. And I'm a prize fighter, yeah!" He showed off some fancy footwork and continued toward her. The combatants were less than ten paces from each other.

A man ran across the street behind the mummy with a coyote hot on his heels. It leapt on his back and pinned him to the ground. Its teeth closed around his neck, silencing his screams.

The animals had made this whole thing even more unpredictable. Somehow, she had the ability to control the minds of these creatures. They had attacked first, overwhelming the hospital with animal bites and stings, and the morgue with corpses partially devoured or bloated with poison. After that, she had descended upon Conestoga with her ultimatum: submit or be destroyed.

Some genius had called the Army, and now their little town had a war on their hands.

But Lanny would put a stop to this madness. He would give this spacefaring, undead monstress a stiff uppercut and a left hook. It would all end now. He would be a champion again; a champion when it really counted.

The fighters stood nearly nose to nose. Her eyes were deep and complex. The contours of her face were like smooth stone, devoid of any flaws. Under other circumstances, it would be a shame to ruin such a face.

Lanny backed up and threw a jab.

Every bone in his left hand shattered. The pain was beyond anything he had felt in the ring or any pulled muscle from a hard day in the mines. He screamed and clutched his destroyed extremity to his chest. He looked up at the Star Mummy like a child struck by their parent for the first time.

She reached for his face and clutched him by the forehead. Her forefinger and thumb dug into his temples. Her palm blazed with white fire.

Lanny Walker suffocated on the stench of his body melting from the inside out.

7

"We're so close," Miles said.

From his house a few miles outside Conestoga, Jessica could hear the bedlam from town. The screams, gunfire, and concussive explosions reminded her of a war movie playing on a loud television, only she knew everything she heard now was real. People were dying in her town—people she saw nearly every day.

"I just hope we're not too late," she said.

After Andrew showed up on her lawn the other night and subsequently turned to dust, her father had tried calming her down enough so she could tell him what happened.

Unsurprisingly, he didn't believe her. She couldn't exactly blame him this time, though. If the positions were somehow reversed, she would've thought her father had finally lost his mind thanks to taking one too many shots to the head during his fighting days.

Her mother didn't believe her either, but at least her mother had convinced her father to go to the police.

Of course, they thought she was hysterical too. She'd been made to repeat her story over and over, asked if she had taken any illegal drugs, and then simply sent her home to get some rest. They treated her like a common drunk or a madwoman.

Before the Star Mummy showed up in town demanding submission and threatening destruction, no one had taken her seriously except for Miles Cutter. He lived on the far edge of the town limits and had the reputation of an adventurer. Rumor had it that he not only had an acute understanding of the sciences, but he also engaged in a variety of occult practices—everything from alchemy to communing with the spirits of the dead. She had come to him with her wild story because he had always treated her kindly, and if anyone would believe such an outlandish tale, it would be him.

Now, the fate of Conestoga, perhaps the entire world, depended on her and her enigmatic friend.

"Just a few more minutes," he said. "Just a few more minutes, and we're there."

He was standing beside a massive contraption that was connected to a bunch of tubes and wires. Its domed body nearly took up the entire room. A square screen on its front showed the phonetic spelling of the words translated from the inscription on the Star Mummy's tomb.

Jessica faced the window, looking down at Conestoga. Another mushroom of fire burst up from its streets.

"Do we even have that long?" she asked.

"I'm well aware that time is of the essence, Jessica. We may not have time to save Conestoga, but at the very least, we might be able to save the world."

She spun to face him. Heat flared in her cheeks.

"But Conestoga is my home. It's your home too."

He looked down and gave his head a small shake.

"It's never been kind to me," he said.

That was true. From the day he arrived in Conestoga, he had been treated like an outcast. He had come here to live a quiet life, but between the condemnation by Father Flavian at St. Gregory's for doing "the devil's work" and getting called a crackpot in the Conestoga Courier Times, he'd experienced anything but. He often told Jessica that if not for their friendship, he would've moved on a long time ago. Still...

"You can't just let these people die!"

A flash of rare anger crossed his face, and he smacked the hull of the machine.

"I can't make this thing work any faster."

He bit his lip and turned once again to the window. Another boom from her dying town heralded the collapse of the courthouse. The once proud building crumbled like a sandcastle in the wind and was replaced with an opaque cloud of dust and smoke.

"Dear God..." she muttered.

Alice pushed open the back door to the malt shop. The alley where she had spent too many smoke breaks to count now looked like something out of a nightmare. The air was thick with dust and smoke. Blood smears adorned the wall of the opposite building. A charred skeleton lay in a partially melted pile of garbage bags. A large bird of prey chewed on a toddler-sized wad of meat pinned under its talons. The meat may have once been a small child, but it no longer resembled one.

Seeing this place of reprieve from her work transformed into a hotbed of death and destruction threw her mind for a loop. She froze in place, her goal of escape forgotten.

Someone grabbed her shoulder. She spun to face Marty. His eyes were wet and pink.

"We have to keep moving," he said.

"Jesus," Josiah said when he saw the scene outside. "We should just..." He looked over his shoulder, back inside the malt shop.

"It's not safe," Alice repeated. As if on cue, the heavy chop-chop-chop of military helicopters sounded in the not too far off distance. "We need to get to the schoolhouse before they turn our town into one big a parking lot."

One of the other survivors whimpered behind her. More gunfire and growling sounded from somewhere nearby. Someone screamed. Something crashed.

Alice and the others headed into the alley, going north toward the only place in town with a bomb shelter.

"It's done!" Miles declared, as if the alarm bells and blinking lights on his oversize machine hadn't made it crystal clear.

Jessica looked out the window. Smoke billowed from various places across the town. Off in the distance, three helicopters were approaching. They looked heavily armed.

"We have to hurry," she said.

The machine spat out a sheet of paper with the phonetic spelling of the inscription's English translation. It was an incantation, a banishing spell to send that Star Mummy back into her tomb.

She hoped it would work. Miles had said it should, but she had a hard time believing that this hunk of plastic and cables could properly decipher a language from outer space. Even though he'd reassured her that the glyphs on the sarcophagus were strikingly similar to the written language of the ancient Sumerians, she had her doubts.

They left Miles' room and got into his Pontiac Chieftain. He gunned the engine, and they headed toward town. It was like driving directly into the heart of Hell itself, a fool's errand, but they had to try. They had to save her home.

Arty Boyer clutched his heart while he hoofed it from the no longer viable hiding place behind the dumpster. The women were several paces ahead, in far better shape than he. His blood pumped overtime, and his breath rushed raggedly in and out.

The Star Mummy was levitating again. Lanny Walker had been reduced to a lumpy pool of pink and yellow fluid.

He didn't even know where he and the others could go. Nowhere was safe, it seemed. Either the Star Mummy found them or one of her animal minions did. He had wound up out in the open after nearly a dozen rattlesnakes spilled out of the vent in his office. It was a goddamn miracle he'd survived that ordeal. If he dropped dead from a heart attack after all this, he'd be one pissed-off, restless spirit. God, if there were such an animal, would have a lot to answer for; the sanctimonious fucker already did, as far as Arty was concerned. Setting loose a seemingly all-powerful space mummy on a small desert town—what kind of divine asshole lets something like that happen?

Another stab of pain in his chest slowed his gait further. He winced and lurched forward. His legs felt like they were underwater. The sensation reminded him of trying to run in a dream.

Something encircled his left ankle and pulled taut. He fell face-forward. His hands went up to brace himself, but they landed in something wet and slid forward, leaving his face unprotected. He landed in the open guts of a discarded torso. The stench was overpowering, suffocating. He flailed and squirmed to try freeing himself. He rolled onto his back. His face and hands were smeared with blood and God only knew what else. A glance down at his ankle showed it ensnared by one of the mummy's bandages.

"Let me go!" he yelled, kicking his girthy legs.

His demands turned to desperate screams as the bandage pulled him toward the levitating figure. It yanked him into the air, dangling him upside down.

"No! *NO!*" he shrieked.

The ground swayed beneath him, already too far below. The women who'd shared the hiding place behind the dumpster were long gone. No one was here to help him. He twisted and kicked, not giving a damn if he plunged head-first onto the pavement. He would rather die that way than...

The bandage snaked further up his leg, constricting his calf and knee. The material burned, scorching the fabric of his trousers.

She would not let him fall. She had something much more dreadful in mind.

Alice and the others came upon the Star Mummy unfurling her bandages to cocoon a man suspended in the air across from her levitating form. He was screaming and thrashing his arms. Steam radiated off the parts of him the bandages covered. Alice could smell the burning meat of the man's flesh.

"Shit!"

"Oh, God," Marty said. "It's Arty Boyer."

The bandages wrapped around the dangling man's belly. The sound of sizzling skin rose in volume and intensity. It reminded Alice of the fry cooker in the malt shop kitchen, and she thought she would never want fried food again.

The now-mummified smoldering form of Arty Boyer plopped to the place where the gutter met the pavement. His body bent in ways bodies weren't supposed to bend, but Alice guessed he was too dead to feel it.

The nude Star Mummy descended gently. Her feet touched down beside a scorpion-riddled corpse. She set her dark sights on Alice and the others.

Josiah stepped forward, wielding a meat cleaver. He must have stolen it from the kitchen on their way out.

"What the hell are you doing, Josiah?" Marty snapped, all rules about profane language now out the window. Josiah ignored him and charged forward. Marty flashed Alice a desperate look. "We have to stop him."

She shook her head. "We need to keep moving."

Josiah got within throwing distance of the mummy as her bandages began to slip off the mangled contours of Arty Boyer. He made a *yuh* sound and chucked the cleaver at her. It was an expert throw. The weapon sailed through the air in a smooth arc, circling as it zeroed in on its target. The blade of the cleaver struck the Star Mummy between the breasts and stuck there.

"Ha-HA!" Josiah whooped.

He faced the others with a prideful grin.

But the Star Mummy remained standing. She plucked the weapon from her chest and no blood poured from the wound. She reared back with the cleaver.

"Look out!" Alice shouted.

The mummy flung it back toward Josiah, who turned to face her once again. By the time he realized what was happening, the cleaver had nearly reached its inevitable target. The blade sliced through Josiah's neck with uncanny precision. Without a word, its wielder called the weapon back. It whipped back into her hand like a boomerang as Josiah dropped to his knees. His head tipped over and fell from the rest of him, hitting the pavement with a wet thump.

The Star Mummy turned her attention toward Alice and the remaining survivors. Her eyes gleamed with bright yellow fire.

8

Earth vs the Star Mummy *will be back after this important message from our sponsor.*

Is your neighbor a commie bastard?

A leering man with dark eyes peers over a hedge at the neighboring house.

Is he controlling your mind?

The man stares into one of the windows at an unsuspecting housewife vacuuming the floor. He places his hands to his temples and closes his eyes. A beam of light emanates from his forehead and enters the window.

Inside, the shaft of light makes gentle contact with the woman's face, then disappears as if she's absorbed it. She blinks and shakes her head. She glares down at the vacuum cleaner before shutting it off.

"I just don't feel like cleaning anymore," she says in a protracted whine.

Is he controlling your television?

She crosses her arms and plops down on the sofa. Her eyes widen with alarm.

The TV shows only a scrambled image. There's nothing discernable on the screen, and its speakers only hiss static.

Is he controlling your bowel movements?

Upstairs, a much less sinister-looking man comes out of the bathroom. As he closes the door, another beam of light from seemingly out of nowhere penetrates his forehead. He winces and clutches his belly. He opens the bathroom door once again and slips inside.

If you answered 'yes,' to any of these questions, contact the New Mexico Department of Communist Concerns at 505-RED-AWAY.

That's 505-733-2929.

We'll investigate, and then eliminate.

We all have a responsibility to keep the communist menace from destroying our way of life. Do your part to preserve America.

Call 505-RED-AWAY.

And remember, Jesus loves you.

Later, the Sonnet Productions Triple Feature Horror Show concludes with a special midnight broadcast of Earth vs the Nudist Camp Freaks. *Make sure your little ones are tucked in and asleep for this one. It's going to get extra freaky when Sonnet Productions brings you* Earth vs the Nudist Camp Freaks. *Showing immediately after* Earth vs the Lava Spiders.

And now, we return with the exciting conclusion of Earth vs the Star Mummy.

9

A dust devil took shape in the middle of Route 63. Miles Cutter didn't slow the Chieftain. As far as he or Jessica could tell, it was simply sand caught up in a small but powerful gust of wind. But then—

Jessica leaned forward and scrunched her brow.

"It's blue," she said.

Miles squinted over the steering wheel to confirm.

"My God," he said.

As the dust thickened, Jessica thought of the other night. She thought of how Andrew's disintegrated bones had blown away on a stiff breeze. The particles then had been blue too. It was the same blue as his chalky features when he first appeared, and it was the same blue as the sand swirling in the middle of the road.

"Stop the car," she said.

"What's that now?"

"Or find some way around it!"

Miles widened his eyes. The circulating particles grew thicker still. The collective mass of them were taking on a human shape.

"Now, Miles!"

Miles jerked the wheel to the right as a face materialized within the churning tongue of sand. It was Andrew's face, and he was smiling at them.

Jessica's secret boyfriend turned herald of the Star Mummy had arrived to thwart their plans. Somehow, he'd known—somehow, his interstellar queen had known. When asked to choose submission or destruction, he'd chosen the former, and now he acted on his subjugator's whims. He would not let Jessica and Miles send her back to her sarcophagus.

The car swerved to his side. It went parallel to Andrew's fluid form. They'd nearly sped past him when a thick tendril of azure sand lashed out and struck the side of the vehicle with a massive thud that was heavier than something any human fist could muster.

The blow sent the car tumbling off the road and into the rocky terrain of the desert. Awful sounds of glass and metal bursting and clanging followed. With impact after impact, pain rocked Jessica's body. She could feel pieces of her breaking apart. She could feel hope slipping away.

As life faded from her, she stole one final glimpse at the already dead Miles and the sheet that contained the translated incantation drifting into the churning blue cloud.

Alice and the others ran for the schoolhouse at the end of Main, and the Star Mummy gave chase. Marty huffed along at a wobbly gallop. He was losing steam. Their numbers had thinned, with some taken out by the mummy herself and others felled by coyotes, snakes, or birds of prey. They still had several paces to go, and even then, they would need to find a way in. The mummy showed no indication of slowing or stalling her pursuit. The helicopters with their murderous payloads were louder now, closer.

There was little of Conestoga left to save. Many familiar sights had been reduced to rubble or engulfed in flames. Bodies filled the streets with a variety of mortal injuries.

Alice's breath rushed in and out. Her leg muscles burned with exertion. She had no plans on what she would do if she managed to survive, especially now that the town where she lived and worked teetered on the brink of obliteration. She wished to survive simply because she could not imagine ceasing to exist. Even with her home and her sole source of income likely gone, she still had possibilities. The breath in her lungs meant boundless potential. She simply had to reach that fallout shelter and find some way to keep that Star Mummy out.

She and the others had nearly reached the school's front stairway when a curtain of cerulean sand blew into their path. The undulating mass was so thick that she couldn't see the schoolhouse behind it. The wall of blue dust housed someone's face. It looked like the McCready boy.

"Andrew?" Marty said in a breathless voice.

On either side of Alice's group, two coyotes padded into view to block any other escape routes. The Star Mummy approached, levitating again and in no hurry. She knew that she had them trapped. It was simply a matter of finishing them off.

The whir of the helicopters was deafening now. A glance upward told her they were almost directly overhead. The Star Mummy looked up to see what Alice had seen, then faced who seemed to be her final targets in the desert town of Conestoga. She locked eyes with Alice and smirked.

Alice screamed, not out of fear, but out of defiance, as the Star Mummy's eyes blazed, and megatons of hell rained down from the sky.

10

We interrupt this program for a breaking news bulletin.

The screen cuts to news reporter Hank Black sitting at his desk. The words *Emergency Bulletin* flash beneath him as he shuffles his papers and adjusts his thick-rimmed glasses. Beads of sweat stand out on his forehead, and he's paler than usual. He clears his throat.

"Good evening," he says. "We've been told that a massive pyramid has materialized in the sky above the New Mexico town of Conestoga. It's green in color and seems to glow. The object is so large that it covers the entire square footage of the town, and its zenith is somewhere above the cloud covering."

"This is not a drill. This is not a hoax. A massive pyramid now hovers over Conestoga, New Mexico. No one seems to know where it came from or how it got here, only that it's large and potentially hostile. There are reports of explosions and gunfire from the town. People have also claimed to have heard screams."

Hank sets his cue cards aside and straightens his tie.

"I'm addressing you now, not as a reporter, but as a man." He licks his lips and swallows. "Do not panic. But I believe this pyramid is a visitor from another world. If that's true, then a reckoning may be upon us—upon our country, upon our world, and upon our species. It's a reckoning that—"

The image on the screen goes fuzzy. Hank's voice warps, rendering his words indecipherable.

When the studio comes back into focus, Hank's appearance has dramatically changed. His tie hangs crooked and the top two buttons of his shirt have come undone. His hair is a mess, sticking up in several directions. Most alarmingly, there's something off about his skin. It's hard to tell on a black-and-white TV, but it seems to have taken on a different skin tone, something gray and unhealthy.

He grins like a patient in the final throes of tetanus, after the lockjaw has set in. His eyes have a bewildered, crazed look to them.

"Sheeeeee's comiiinnngg," he says through his gritted teeth. "Submit or beeee destrooooyyyyed."

He laughs as the screen goes snowy with a burst of static.

Afterword

I hope you enjoyed *Earth vs the Star Mummy*. This story is part of a project I embarked upon with authors Candace Nola and Judith Sonnet. Judith has been doing these ten-day novellas these past few months, meaning that she'll start a book on day one and publish it by day ten, and from what I can tell, she's seen a good deal of success from it.

I found the concept intriguing because I sometimes find it hard to finish things in a satisfactory timeframe. Something like National Novel Writing Month is cool for some, but I've never had much luck with it. Frankly, sticking with one project for a month isn't something my attention span will allow. Ten days, however? That, I can do.

We decided to focus on a shared theme this time around. As the three of us are fans of cheap, 1950s science fiction horror movies, we chose that as our aesthetic. I included commercials for each of their stories in the middle of mine just to break things up a bit and have fun with the concept. If I have one rule I stick to when it comes to this writing stuff, it's that I don't spend time on something unless I'm having fun doing it. Life's too short for that nonsense.

One of the roadblocks on this project I initially faced was that I'd accidentally outlined something that would've been fine in a typical

Lucas Mangum book, meaning I plotted out something a bit more sprawling than the story you just read. Thankfully, I realized early on that in order for this to work (read: if I wanted a story that was properly edited before its release on day ten); I needed to finish the manuscript in more like four to six days. That meant I needed to cut and do so in a creative way, so the story didn't lose any of its narrative beats. It was a cool exercise, and it got me thinking of ways to perfect my already minimalistic approach to storytelling.

I'd like to thank my partner Jean for giving me the space and time to write this story within such a short period, Judith for inspiring this project, Christy Aldrich at Grim Poppy Design for this story's incredible cover, and Candace for coming along for the ride and getting her editors on this story.

Most of all, I would like to thank my mom. Thirty years ago, she turned me onto movies like *THEM!*, *It Came from Beneath the Sea*, *The Blob*, *Invaders from Mars*, and countless others from this era. If not for instilling a love of this media in me at a young age, the story you hold in your hands would simply not exist. I'm not even sure I'd be writing at all if not for her; I certainly wouldn't be writing horror. So, thanks for that, Mom. Love you.

For the rest of you, I really appreciate you giving my work a chance. I'm always so amazed at the readership I've garnered when most of the time I just feel like a big kid playing with some toys or an adult neurotic exorcising some personal demons. It's so gratifying to know you're out there and willing to come along on these strange and sometimes uncomfortable rides.

Take care of yourselves,

Lucas Mangum

Somewhere in Texas, 11/20/2022

About the Author

Lucas Mangum is a Splatterpunk Award nominee for Best Novel (*Pandemonium* with Ryan Harding) and Best Novella (*Saint Sadist*), as well as the author of the cult hit *Gods of the Dark Web* and several other novellas and short stories. With Jeff Burk, he co-hosts *Make Your Own Damn Podcast*, a show dedicated to cult movies. San Diego-born and Philly-raised, he now lives in Austin with his family. Sign up for his newsletter at LucasMangum.com